EARRINGS!

CHILDREN'S BOOKS BY JUDITH VIORST

Sunday Morning
I'll Fix Anthony
Alexander and the Terrible, Horrible,
No Good, Very Bad Day
My Mama Says There Aren't Any Zombies,
Ghosts, Vampires, Creatures, Demons,
Monsters, Fiends, Goblins, or Things
Rosie and Michael
The Tenth Good Thing about Barney
Alexander, Who Used to Be Rich Last Sunday
If I Were in Charge of the World and Other Worries
The Good-Bye Book
Earrings!

EARRINGS!

by JUDITH VIORST

illustrated by Nola Langner Malone

ATHENEUM 1990 NEW YORK

Atheneum
Macmillan Publishing Company
866 Third Avenue, New York, NY 10022
Collier Macmillan Canada, Inc.
First Edition
Printed in the United States of America
10 9 8 7 6 5 4 3 2 1

Library of Congress Cataloging-in-Publication Data
Viorst, Judith.
Earrings! / by Judith Viorst ; illustrated by Nola Langner Malone.
—1st ed.   p.   cm.
Summary: A young girl uses various arguments to try to convince
her parents to let her have her ears pierced.
ISBN 0-689-31615-1
[1. Earrings—Fiction.]   I. Malone, Nola Langner, ill.
II. Title.
PZ7.V816Ear   1990   [E]—dc20
89-17846   CIP   AC

This book is dedicated to
Melissa Hersh and Amy Oberdorfer
(because they got me thinking about pierced ears)
and to
Nancy Gordillo, Susannah Lescher, Elizabeth Pitofsky,
Rebecca Rosenfeld, and Lisa Schorr
(just because)—J. V.

To Marina Rose Musicus,
with love from Grandma—N.L.M.

I want them.
I need them.
I love them.

I've got to have them.

My mom and my dad
won't let me have them.

Earrings.
Beautiful earrings for
Pierced ears.

Teachers and
lady dentists have them.

Mothers and
even grandmothers have them.

Why won't my mom and my dad let me have
Pierced ears?

They say that I'm too young.
I'm not too young.
I'm actually very mature for my age.
I clear the plates after dinner.
I take a shower without even being told.

They say that I need to be patient.
I've tried being patient.
I'm tired of patient.

I want my ears pierced NOW—not when I'm

Twenty

Forty

Eighty

A hundred years old.

I want them. I need them. I love them.
Beautiful earrings. Glorious earrings.

My mom and my dad say,
Wait for a couple of years.

I tell them I'm the only girl
In my class
In my school
In the world
In the solar system
Whose mom and dad won't let her have
Pierced ears.

At your age, they say, pierced ears are premature.
I HATE "premature."

At your age, they say, pierced ears are inappropriate.
I REALLY HATE "inappropriate."

At your age, they say, pierced ears look a little....tacky.
I can't believe I've got such old-fashioned parents!

I want them. I need them. I love them.
Beautiful earrings. Glorious earrings.
My mom and my dad keep saying weird things like,
Why?

Because they'd make me look good.
Because they'd make me feel good.

And because, furthermore, I'd be so proud of wearing them,
I'd stand up straight and hold my head up high.
Which means that they would also be good for my posture.

(And I hear that they keep your earlobes warm in winter.)

My mom and my dad ask,
What do you want for your birthday?
I tell them what I want for my birthday: pierced ears.

My mom and my dad ask,
What do you want for Christmas?
I tell them that I only want pierced ears.

And what do you think I say when they ask me,
What should we bring you back from our vacation?

> I say earrings.
> Beautiful earrings.
> Glorious earrings.
> Beautiful, glorious earrings for
> Pierced ears.

Instead of earrings, they say,
We could get you a locket.
I don't WANT a locket.
Instead of earrings, they say,
We could get you a charm bracelet.
I REALLY don't want a charm bracelet.

As a substitute for earrings, they say,
We brought you back this....
Don't they understand?
There *isn't* any substitute for earrings!

I want them.
I need them.
I love them.
Beautiful earrings.
Glorious earrings.

I argue and beg and sometimes there's yelling and tears.

I tell my mom and my dad all the things I would do
If only
If only
If only
If only
If only they would let me have pierced ears:

Like, walk our dog every day for one whole year.

Like, clean up my room every day for one whole year.

Like, read a book once a week for one whole year.

Like, be nice to my little brother for one whole year.
Well, maybe six months.

And I wouldn't ask for new clothes, because I could wear the same old clothes—and just change my earrings.

I want them.
I need them.
I love them.

I keep telling my mom and my dad I've got to have them.
My mom and my dad say they're tired of hearing this stuff.

But I promise
I promise
I promise

I cross-my-heart promise that they'll never hear it again,
The minute they decide I'm old enough

For earrings.
Beautiful earrings.

Glorious earrings.

Beautiful, glorious earrings for
Pierced ears.